THE DARK KNIGHT

SUPER DC HEROES

THE BLACK MASQUERADE

WRITTEN BY
SEAN TULIEN

ILLUSTRATED BY
LUCIANO VECCHIO

BATMAN CREATED BY BOB KANE

STONE ARCH BOOKS
a capstone imprint

PUBLISHED BY STONE ARCH BOOKS IN 2013
A CAPSTONE IMPRINT
1710 ROE CREST DRIVE
NORTH MANKATO, MN 56003
WWW.CAPSTONEPUB.COM

CATALOGING-IN-PUBLICATION DATA IS AVAILABLE AT THE
LIBRARY OF CONGRESS WEBSITE.

ISBN: 978-1-4342-4486-4 (LIBRARY BINDING)
ISBN: 978-1-4342-4824-4 (PAPERBACK)

SUMMARY: BRUCE WAYNE'S MASQUERADE BALL FOR CHARITY
IS CRASHED BY NONE OTHER THAN THE BLACK MASK. HE
AND FALSE FACE SOCIETY MEMBERS ROB THE GUESTS,
STEAL THE CHARITABLE DONATIONS, AND THEN KIDNAP
COMMISSIONER GORDON. WITHOUT THE COMMISSIONER'S
HELP, THE DARK KNIGHT IS LEFT TO TAKE ON THE ENTIRE
CRIMINAL UNDERWORLD ON HIS OWN.

ART DIRECTOR: BOB LENTZ
DESIGNER: BRANN GARVEY

PRINTED IN THE UNITED STATES OF AMERICA
IN NORTH MANKATO, MINNESOTA.

TABLE OF CONTENTS

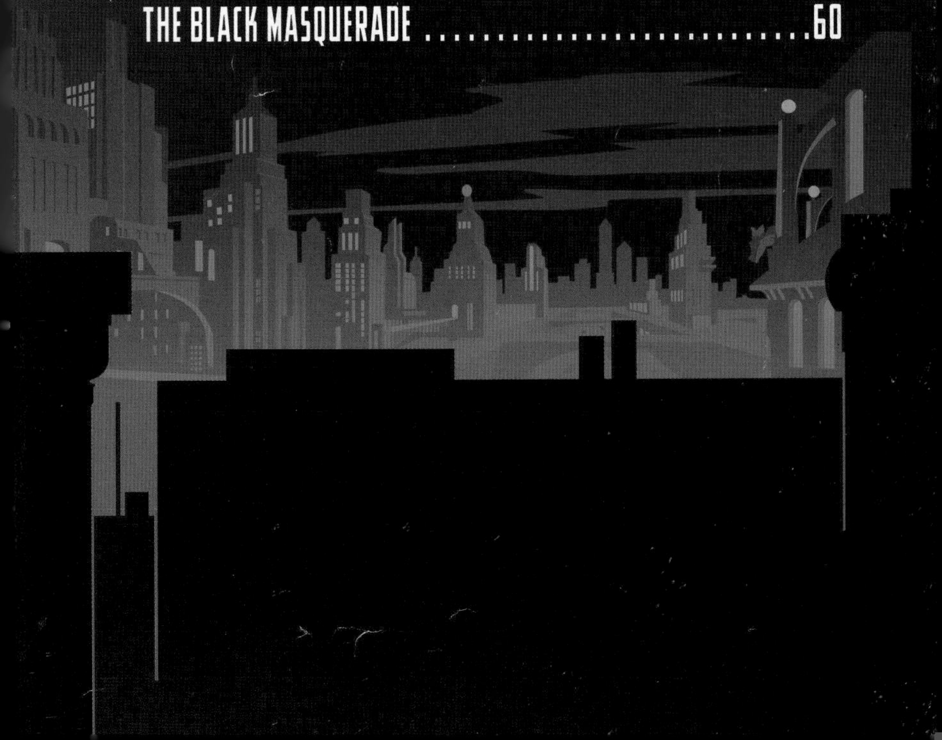

WHILE STILL A BOY, BRUCE WAYNE WITNESSED THE BRUTAL MURDER OF HIS PARENTS. THE TRAGIC EVENT CHANGED THE YOUNG BILLIONAIRE FOREVER. BRUCE VOWED TO RID GOTHAM CITY OF EVIL AND KEEP ITS PEOPLE SAFE FROM CRIME. AFTER YEARS OF TRAINING HIS BODY AND MIND, HE DONNED A NEW UNIFORM AND A NEW IDENTITY.

HE BECAME...

THE
DARK KNIGHT
™

CHAPTER 1

MISSING MASK

CHING! Two-Face flipped his coin into the air with his thumb. The metallic sound echoed through the cool night. ***CHING!*** ***CHING!*** He flipped the coin again and again. His patience was wearing thin.

"Would you please stop tossing that cursed coin of yours, Two-Face?" the Penguin chirped. "It's driving me cuckoo."

Two-Face grunted, then carefully pocketed his precious coin. He pulled back his coat sleeve and checked his watch.

"Where is Black Mask?" Two-Face growled. "He was supposed to be here by 6:30, and it's nearly a quarter past seven."

The Penguin scanned the area, taking in all of the assorted criminals he and Two-Face commanded. There were at least thirty hardened crooks and thugs there, all of them loyal to their respective bosses. But Black Mask and his masked henchmen hadn't arrived yet.

"I admit," Penguin began, "I am concerned. This meeting was Black Mask's idea, so there's no reason he'd be late. Unless . . ."

A sinister scowl crawled across the Penguin's lips. He glared at Two-Face. "I smell a rat," he croaked.

Two-Face reached out and grabbed the Penguin by his collar with both hands.

"Who you callin' a rat, bird-brain?!" Two-Face yelled, lifting the villain off the ground.

AWK! AWK! The Penguin squawked and squirmed under the stronger man's grip. Several members of the Penguin's gang stepped forward, raising their fists. Seeing this, Two-Face's men stepped up as well.

As Two-Face glanced at the advancing troops, the Penguin kicked Two-Face in the kneecap with the heel of his boot.

"OW!" Two-Face yelled.

The Penguin scrambled free from Two-Face and then pointed his umbrella at him. "Get him!" he cried.

A moment later, both of the gangsters' crews were battling in an all-out brawl.

SMACK! POW! SLAM!

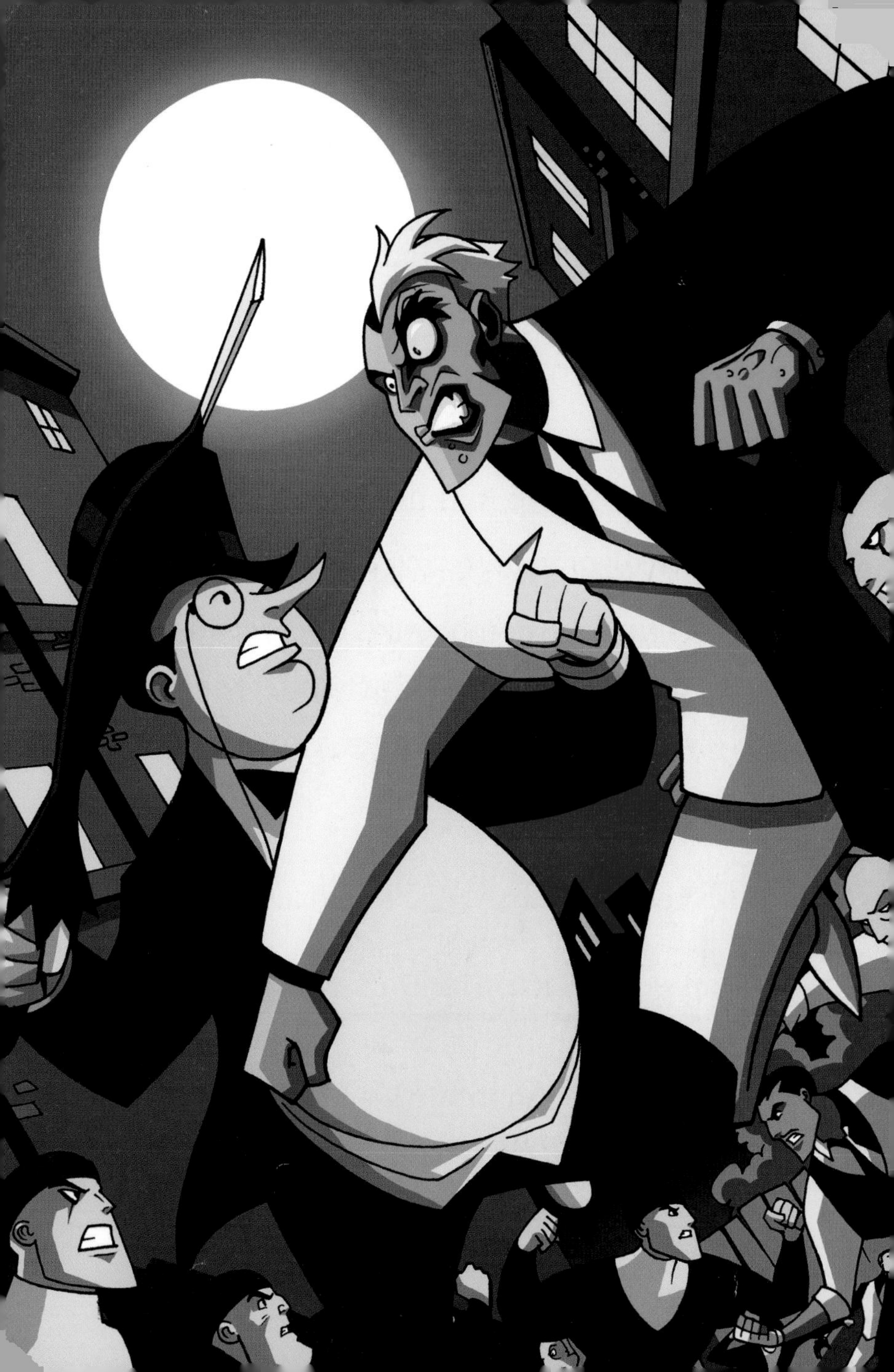

From the cover of a nearby rooftop, the Dark Knight watched the madness unfold. He scanned the horizon, looking for Black Mask and his men. "I can't wait any longer," the hero said to himself.

Batman threw himself off the rooftop and soared down to join the fight.

CLICK-SNAP! The Dark Knight flipped down his night-vision goggles and activated them. Speeding toward the ground, the hero aimed himself directly for Two-Face and the Penguin.

Below, the criminals were too busy punching and kicking each other to notice Batman's approach. The Dark Knight watched through the amplified view of his goggles as the Penguin pressed a button on his umbrella. *CLICK!* A blade popped out of the tip.

"You've really ruffled my feathers now, Harvey," the Penguin said. "There will be no alliance between our gangs!"

"We both know that I'm the king of Gotham City's underworld!" Two-Face growled.

The Penguin cackled. "You're the king, eh?" he said. "Even if that were true, that would make you my subject . . . because I'm the emperor!" He dashed toward Two-Face with his weapon raised.

THUD! Batman's boots smashed into the Penguin's side. He fell to the ground clutching his ribs.

The Dark Knight rolled to his feet. "Hello, Harvey," the hero said to Two-Face.

"Who invited this winged rodent?" Two-Face snarled.

By now, the fighting henchmen had taken notice of Batman's arrival. As Two-Face and Batman circled each other, the thugs began to surround the Dark Knight.

Two-Face grinned, curling his hands into fists and raising them to his chin. "You're outnumbered, Bats."

"Am I?" Batman asked.

KA·THOK! KA·THOK! Suddenly, two floodlights bathed the scene in blinding light.

Everyone froze and shielded their eyes as a megaphone cut through the silence. "This is Commissioner Gordon of the Gotham City Police! You're surrounded! Now put your weapons down — and your hands up!"

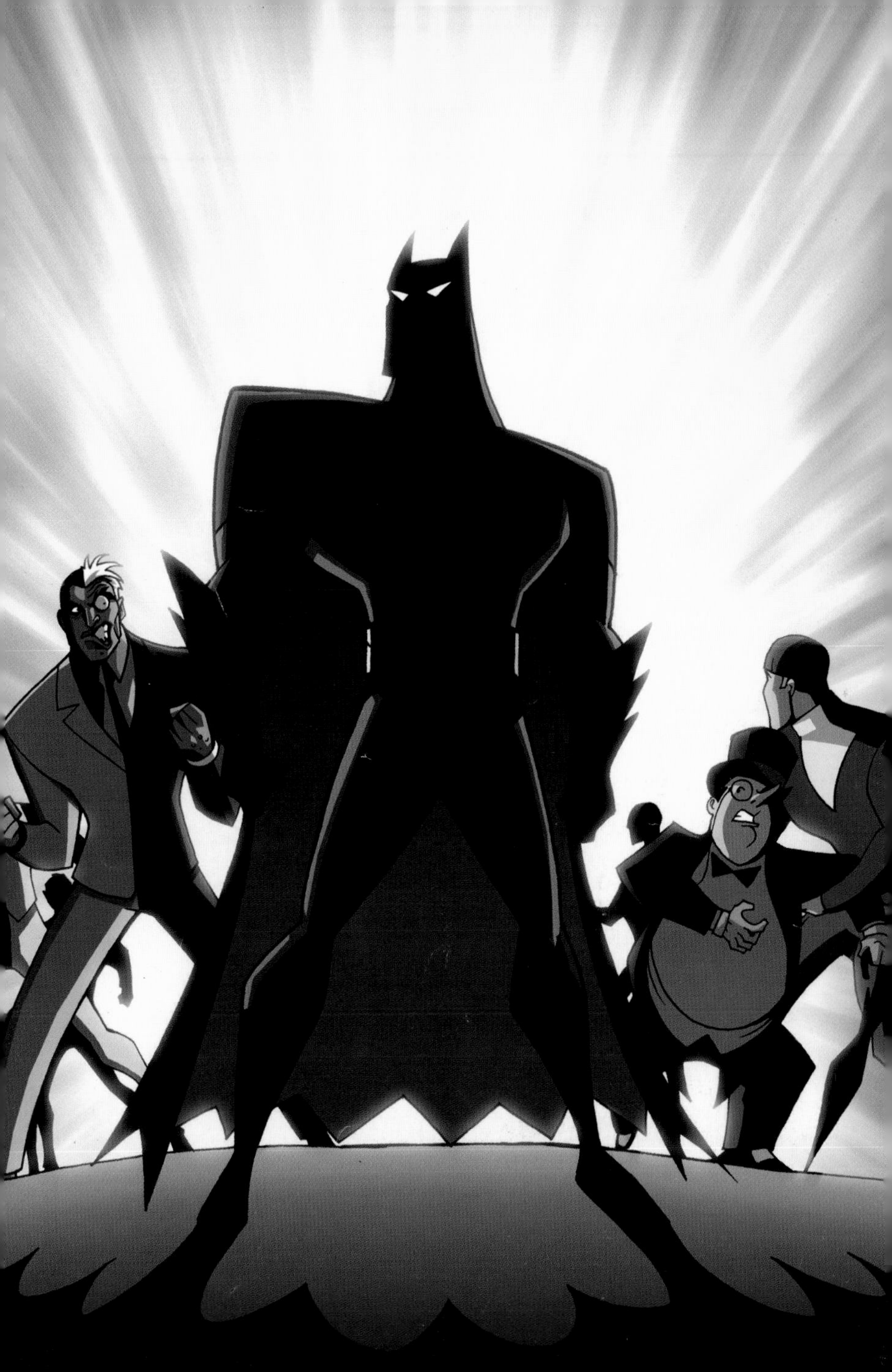

Seeing the large police force, Two-Face's men turned and ran. Penguin's men immediately followed suit.

"Cowards!" Two-Face cried. "Stand and fight!" Several men turned back to look, but none of them stopped.

Batman used a zip-tie to secure the Penguin's hands behind his back. The villain wiggled back and forth on the ground, attempting to flip over. "Help me, Two-Face!"

Two-Face scowled. He turned to flee — but a Batarang with a rope attached to it wrapped around his legs.

Two-Face fell on the ground with a **THUMP!** Before he could recover, Batman had the villain's hands tied behind his back. "This isn't over," Two-Face said coolly.

Batman lifted Two-Face to his feet and guided him toward a police vehicle. He and Commissioner Gordon carefully deposited the two villains into separate squad cars.

Moments later, Gordon's men returned with several handcuffed henchmen.

"We managed to catch a few," one of Gordon's lieutenants said.

Gordon nodded. "Nicely done. With their testimony, we'll be able to put Two-Face and the Penguin behind bars for a while." Gordon turned to face Batman. "Not bad for a night's work, huh?"

"It would've been better if we got Black Mask, too," Batman said.

Gordon rubbed his chin. "Agreed," he said. "Do you think Black Mask somehow got wind of our stakeout and bailed?"

"Almost certainly, Jim," Batman said. "In fact, I'd bet he's the one who phoned in the anonymous tip to you about the meeting itself."

Gordon frowned. "But why?"

"With Two-Face and the Penguin out of commission," Batman said, "their thugs will be looking for work. And Black Mask will be all too happy to add them to his False Face Society."

"So we've handed Gotham's underworld over to Black Mask on a silver platter," Gordon said dryly.

Batman nodded. "That's why I wanted to get all three at once."

Gordon sighed. "What do we do now?"

Before Batman could answer, a voice spoke through his secret earpiece.

"Master Bruce," came Alfred's voice. "It would be impolite to be late for your own party, you know."

"I have to go," Batman said to Gordon.

"It's all right," Gordon said. "I have to be somewhere, too. Bruce Wayne invited me to a masquerade ball for charity."

"Wayne, huh?" Batman said, choosing his words very carefully. Gordon was a clever man, and the last thing the Dark Knight wanted was to reveal that he and Wayne were the same person.

Gordon shrugged. "He may be an egotistical billionaire," he said, "but deep down he's a good man who likes helping others. A lot like you, really."

More than you know, Jim, Batman thought.

CHAPTER 2

THE MASQUERADE BALL

The Batmobile raced down the streets of Gotham City. Batman's thoughts were racing, too. Black Mask was cold, more calculating, and far less sane than the Penguin or Two-Face. The thought of that maniac controlling all of the criminals in Gotham made Batman's skin crawl.

But his responsibilities at Wayne Manor made him just as uncomfortable. Bruce was no stranger to wearing a mask. He did so as Batman each night, and as Bruce Wayne during the day.

But this evening would be different. Tonight he'd be wearing a mask on top of the one he wore as Bruce Wayne.

The Batmobile pulled into Wayne Manor through its secret entrance. Batman jumped out. His boots landed softly on the ground just a few feet from his butler.

"Right on time, as always, Master Bruce," Alfred said. The butler held out a tuxedo and a pair of shiny black shoes. "But I brought your attire for the evening with me — just in case."

Batman quickly removed his mask to reveal the face of Bruce Wayne. A warm smile crossed his lips. "Thank you, Alfred," he said, taking the clothes. "Has my date for the evening arrived yet?"

"Indeed," Alfred said. "I'll tell Selina you'll meet her shortly."

Bruce quickly put on his tux, but began to struggle with his bow tie. "You'd think I would've gotten the hang of these things by now," he mumbled.

Alfred let out a good-natured sigh. "I admit, Master Bruce," he said, "it amazes me that you can fling about those Batarangs of yours, but the simple function of a bow tie continues to elude you." The butler's nimble fingers busied themselves with Bruce's bow tie. "There."

Bruce smiled. "What would I do without you, Alfred?"

"Oh, I'm sure you'd manage somehow," Alfred said. "I will alert your guests that you have arrived."

Bruce nodded. Alfred began to walk up the steps that led up from the Batcave to Wayne Manor's main floor.

Then Alfred stopped and turned to face Bruce. "Oh, one last thing," he said, producing a mask from inside his tux. "I had this made for you to wear tonight."

Alfred tossed the mask to Bruce. "Thank you, Alfred," Bruce said. "It's perfect."

Bruce lifted the mask over his face and glanced at his reflection in the computer screens. The ball he was hosting would have Gotham City's elite citizens in attendance. They would wine, dine, don playful masks — and donate large sums of money to the Children's Charity of Gotham City.

"You were wise to choose a mask that looks nothing like Batman's," Bruce said.

Alfred nodded. "If anyone could make the connection between Bruce Wayne and Batman, it would be Selina Kyle."

Bruce had invited Selina to be his date for a reason. While Bruce disapproved of her habit of robbing the rich to give to the poor, he had to admit that she, too, was helping Gotham in her own way.

However, Catwoman committed crimes to help others while Batman fought to enforce the law. Her motives were moral, but her actions weren't. Bruce hoped that Catwoman would someday realize that the ends don't always justify the means. Until then, as Bruce Wayne, he'd keep her close and hope his actions would rub off on her.

And if not, Bruce thought, *at least I can keep my eye on her.*

All the thought of double identities and masks began to make his head spin. He did his best to put on Bruce's famous smile behind his mask.

Then Bruce and Alfred began the long walk up the stairs to join the masquerade.

* * *

Alfred swung open the double doors to the ballroom in dramatic fashion and announced Bruce Wayne to his guests. They cheered wildly for the generous billionaire.

"Thank you, thank you," Bruce said, with every ounce of his charisma. "But I should be applauding you folks for your donations this evening. With your help, we will make a difference in thousands of children's lives here in Gotham."

Deflecting the attention onto the crowd was an old trick to Bruce, and once again it worked like a charm. The audience cheered even louder after hearing they played a part in something great. Bruce waved, then slipped into the crowd.

As Bruce passed Commissioner Gordon, he stopped to chat. "I heard about your big bust this evening," Bruce said, patting Gordon on the back. "It's comforting to know there will be two fewer criminal masterminds running wild."

Gordon smiled. "I think another man deserves most of the credit . . ." He placed a bat-like mask on his face. ". . . Batman!"

Bruce laughed. He grabbed two glasses of champagne from a nearby waiter and handed one to Gordon. "To your — and Batman's — successes!" he said.

CLINK!

Bruce and Gordon tapped their glasses together.

"Cheers," Gordon said, then left to mingle.

He wears a mask well, Bruce thought. *But I can tell he's uneasy.*

Bruce glanced at the donation box. It was filled to the brim with cash donations. Two of Bruce's security officers stood guard next to it. While Bruce didn't expect any disruptions this evening, so much money in one place would be a tempting target for any crook.

A sleek arm slipping under the crook of Bruce's elbow interrupted his thoughts. "Hello, Bruce," Selina purred. "Let's see that mask of yours." Selina's deft hand slowly turned Bruce to face her.

Bruce grinned when he saw she was wearing a Catwoman mask. "Interesting choice of mask," he said, taking Selina's hand.

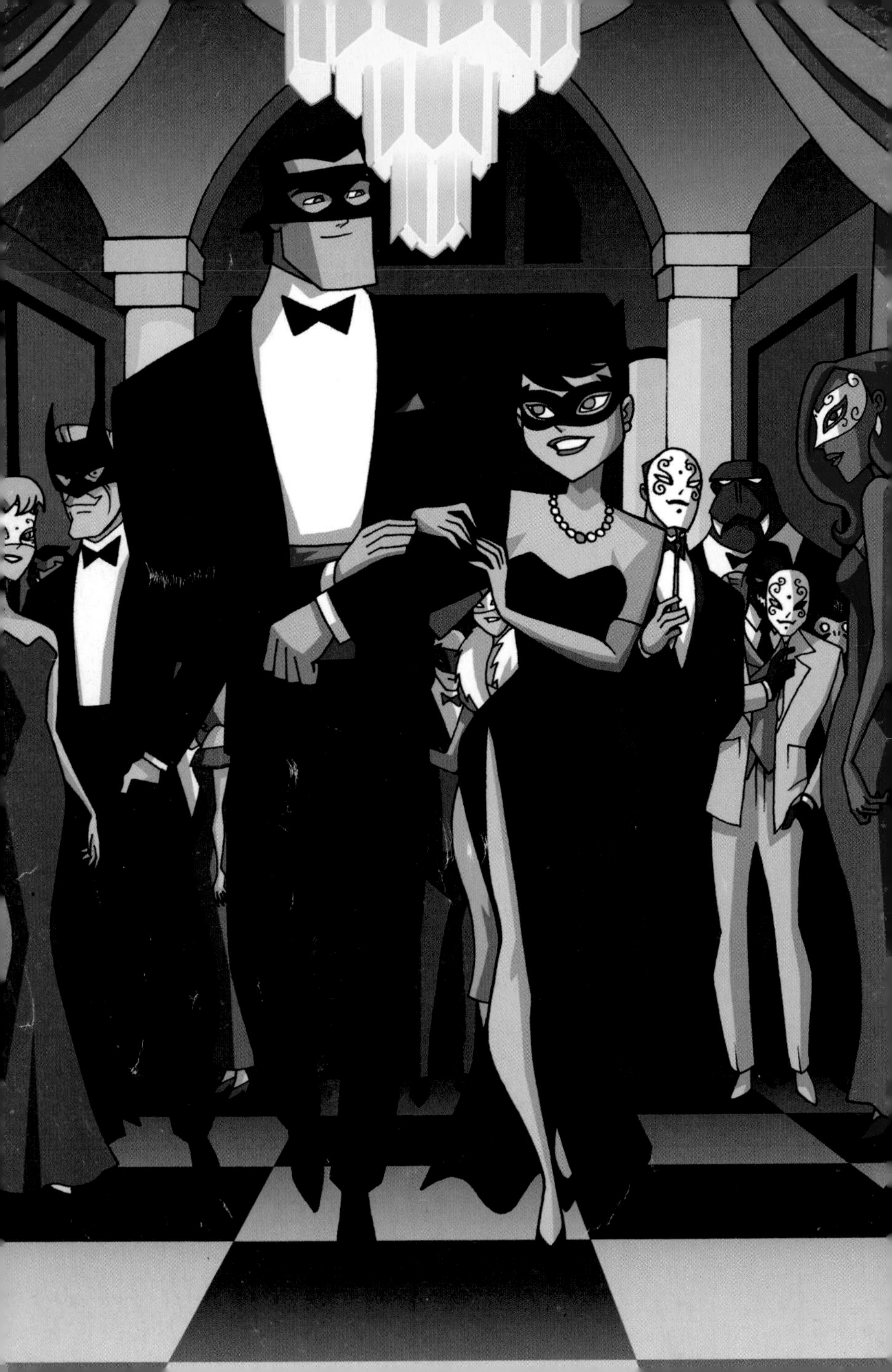

"As is yours," Selina said. "May I ask why you went with this one?"

Bruce shrugged. "You'll have to ask my butler," he said. "What about you?"

"Isn't it obvious?" Selina said with a sly grin. She raised her hands up like a pouncing feline. "I'm Catwoman!"

Bruce chuckled. "I can see the resemblance," he said. "After all, you both have a soft spot for orphans."

"Just like you, too," Selina agreed. She glanced around the room.

"Quite a turnout," Selina said. "And from the looks of it, they're pretty wealthy."

Bruce glanced around. Most of the guests were wearing the white masks that he and Alfred had sent with the invitations. Only a few had chosen their own masks.

"Honestly," Selina said. "It's a little silly that they have to be wined and dined to spread the wealth. I mean, how much money does one person need — especially when so many innocent children are homeless and hungry?"

Bruce nodded. "It is a shame that more people don't donate money," he admitted. "But it's theirs to do with as they please."

Selina grinned. "Well, you know what they say," she said, sliding her arms around Bruce's shoulders. "Possession is nine-tenths of the law."

Bruce's eyes narrowed. "Are you implying they should be robbed?" he asked. "You know I don't support criminal acts."

Selina frowned. "If you ask me, having so much money to oneself *is* criminal."

Bruce was about to respond when something caught his eye. "Please excuse me for a moment, Selina," he said.

Selina placed her hands on her hips. "Was it something I said?"

"Not at all," Bruce replied, flashing his billionaire smile. "I look forward to continuing this conversation."

Selina pouted. "I'll be waiting."

Bruce made his way through the sea of guests toward a man wearing two masks. As Bruce approached the man, Bruce said, "I couldn't help but admire both of your masks from across the way."

The man tilted his head. "Both masks?" he asked. "I'm only wearing one."

Bruce frowned. He removed his mask and confidently thrust out his open hand.

"I don't believe we've met," Bruce said. "I'm Bruce Wayne."

The man didn't shake Bruce's hand. "What kind of host takes off his mask at a masquerade?" the man asked. "Isn't the point to try to puzzle out who is whom?"

"True," Bruce said pleasantly. "I suppose that means I'll have to guess your identity?"

The man shook his head. "Don't bother, Mr. Wayne," he said.

Slowly, the man lowered his white mask. "There, my mask is off," the man said. "Do you recognize me now?"

The hairs on Bruce's neck stood up as the man laughed. It was a cold but quiet chuckle. One Bruce had never heard — but one that Batman was very familiar with.

"Black Mask," Bruce said, trying to sound more frightened than he really was. "What are you doing here?"

"What do you think?" was the villain's cryptic response.

"It's nice to see you, Black Mask," Gordon said, interrupting. He stepped out from the crowd and removed his Batman mask. "I just missed you earlier, and I was afraid I wouldn't catch up with you."

"Just the man I'm looking for," Black Mask said with a grin.

Bruce didn't like where this was headed. He started to form a plan when he noticed that Selina was sneaking up behind Black Mask. His sharp eyes spotted a small, dime-sized object in her hands. *That must be a tracking device*, Bruce realized. *Very clever, Selina.*

Black Mask snapped his fingers. *CLICK!* Several masked men stepped forward. Each of their masks were different, but they all had a sinister look to them.

False Facers! Bruce realized. One of them was the Penguin's former right hand man. Another was Two-Face's former captain. They guarded Black Mask on all sides.

Selina can't get to him now, Bruce thought. Bruce stepped forward, putting himself right between Gordon and Black Mask. The False Facers behind Black Mask stepped closer — and away from his rear. *Just a little farther,* Bruce thought.

Bruce took one more step. Black Mask's thugs stepped between Bruce and Black Mask, leaving the rear unguarded. Bruce leaned in close to the villain. "This doesn't need to come to violence," Bruce whispered.

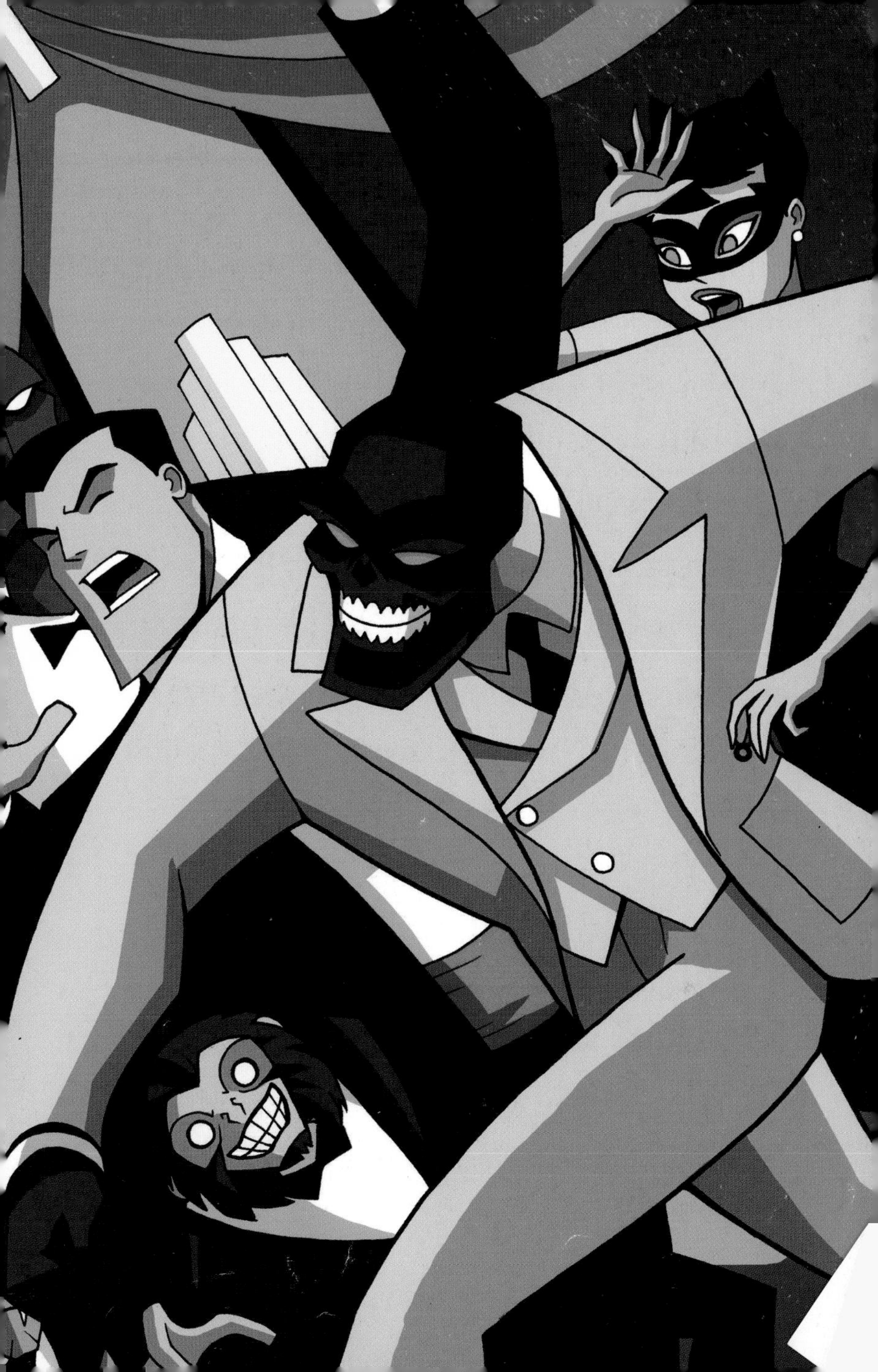

SMACK! Black Mask rammed his fist into Bruce's jaw. Bruce fell to the floor in a heap, pretending to be unconscious — but not before he saw Selina slip the tracking device onto Black Mask's shoulder. She then walked away, unnoticed.

The guests who hadn't already left were running out the doors. That just left Gordon and the two donation box security guards.

Black Mask cracked his knuckles. "These rich guys can never take a punch," he said. He nodded at his men. "Boys, get to it."

The False Facers attacked Gordon and the guards. Bruce, meanwhile, continued to play possum. Every part of him ached to help his friend, Gordon, as well as the two guards. But as Bruce Wayne, there was nothing he could do.

Soon, Black Mask's men overwhelmed Gordon and the guards. All three lay unconscious on the marble floor.

Black Mask gestured toward the donation box. "Grab that," he told his men.

CRACK! One of his men pried off the lock with a crowbar. Two other False Facers lifted it up and began to carry it outside.

Black Mask glanced at the cash-filled box, then to the unconscious Police Commissioner. "Cold, hard cash, and more of my competition eliminated," he said. "Now that's what I call a two-for-one!"

Two of the False Facers grabbed Gordon by the shoulders and pulled him out the door. Black Mask grinned, turned on his heel, and left with the rest of his men.

CHAPTER 3

MIXED SIGNALS

Back in the Batcave, Bruce tapped away at the Batcomputer as Alfred dabbed Bruce's jaw with some antiseptic. "I hope you had a good reason for taking that punch," Alfred said.

"It had to look real," Bruce said.

Alfred nodded. "I'd say you succeeded," he said. "So where do you suppose Black Mask has taken Commissioner Gordon?"

Bruce rubbed his jaw. "I have no idea," he said. "But I know someone who does."

"Selina, I presume?" Alfred asked.

Bruce smiled. "Nothing escapes you, Alfred," he said. He brought up Catwoman's file on the Batcomputer. "I saw her stick a tracking device to Black Mask's suit. That's why I took that punch — to provide her with a distraction."

Alfred tucked away the medical kit. "Well played," he said. "But how will you locate Catwoman? She's hard to find."

Bruce shrugged. "Got any bright ideas?"

Alfred arched an eyebrow. "One, in fact. How does Gordon get a hold of the Dark Knight when the police require his help?"

Bruce smiled. "Brilliant."

* * *

Moments later, Batman stood in front of the Bat-Signal atop the roof of the Gotham City Police Department.

Batman reached into his Utility Belt and pulled out a roll of electrical tape. He ripped off a few pieces, then carefully stuck them to the Bat-Signal.

"That should do it," he said. He flipped the switch. *CLICK!*

Batman lifted his eyes to the dark, cloudy skies. Looming just beneath the full moon was a silhouette of a cat.

"How's it look, Alfred?" Batman asked through his radio earpiece.

"Purr-fect," Alfred said.

Batman chuckled.

"Something funny?" came a voice from behind him.

Batman tensed and turned. When he saw Catwoman perched nearby, he relaxed. "That was fast," he said.

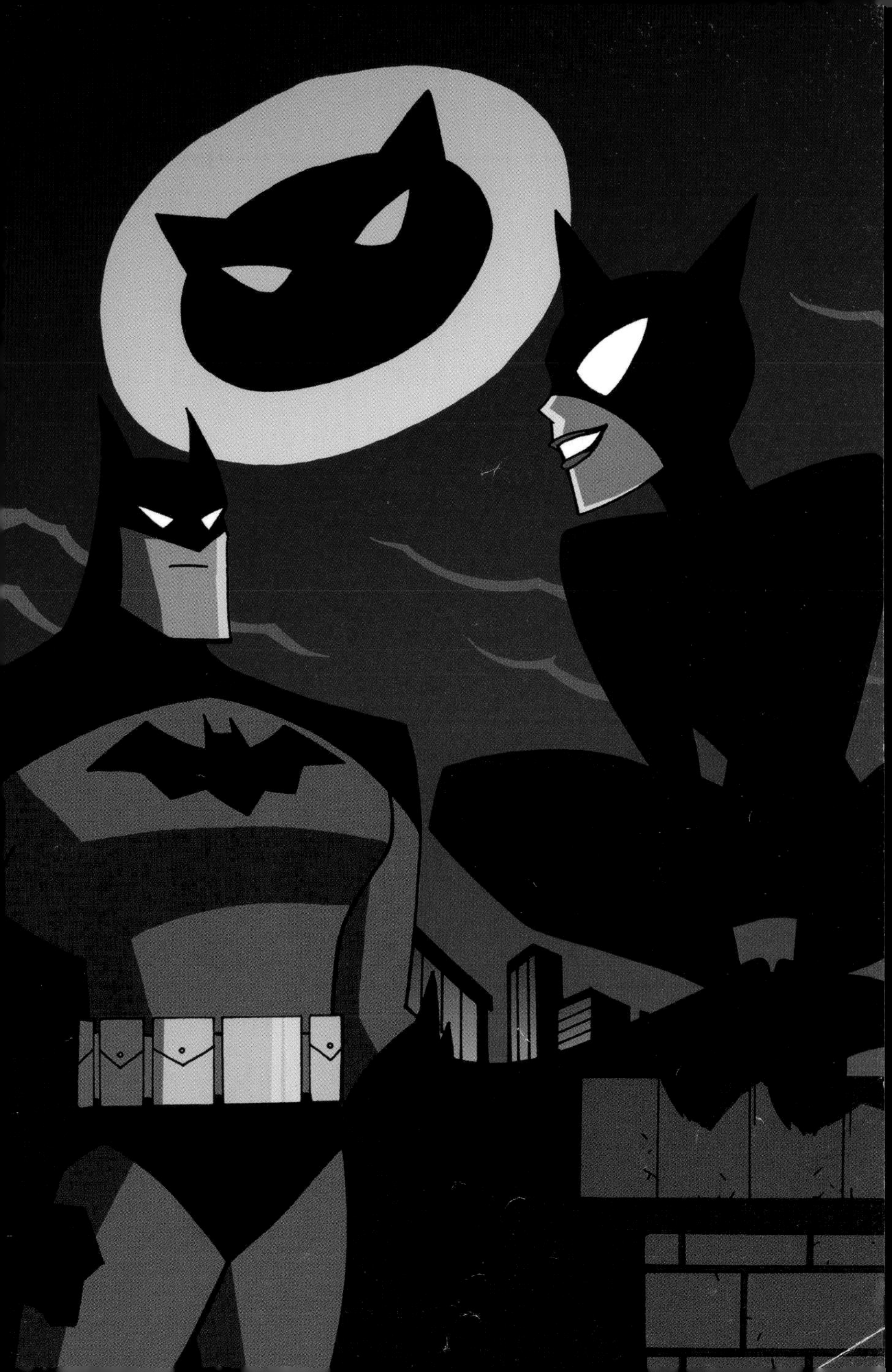

"I was already in the neighborhood," Catwoman said. "Earlier this evening, I was on a promising date with a very eligible bachelor." She pounced down to Batman's level and approached him. "But I'd much rather prowl the streets with you."

Batman arched an eyebrow. "Not interested."

"Oh?" she said, glancing up at the sky. "I guess I'm picking up some mixed signals, then. Care to clarify?"

"I don't know if you've heard," Batman said, "but a large sum of money intended for the city's orphans was stolen from Wayne Manor."

"I did hear about that," Catwoman said flatly. "In fact, this little meeting of ours interrupted my search."

Good, Batman thought. "Any leads?"

Catwoman crossed her arms. "Why should I share?"

"You want the money back for the orphans," Batman said with a shrug, "and I want to rescue Gordon. I'd say our objectives line up perfectly — in this case."

"So where's the Boy Wonder?" Catwoman asked. "Super hero summer school?"

"I need someone familiar with sneaking around in the shadows," Batman said.

Catwoman smirked. "You mean . . . little old me?"

"Why not?" Bruce asked. "And since you were once an orphan yourself, I figure you'll be motivated to help recover the stolen donations."

Catwoman's eyes seemed to glimmer. She uncrossed her arms. "Okay," she said. "But we do things my way. Deal?"

Batman shifted uncomfortably. He needed Selina's intel. "Fair enough," he said. "So where's Black Mask?"

"Gotham Cemetery," Catwoman said.

"How do you know that?" Batman asked, doing his best to sound surprised.

Catwoman smirked. "Catch me if you can," she said, then leaped off the rooftop. **CRACK!** Her whip attached to a nearby building, and she swung away.

* * *

A short time later, Batman and Catwoman arrived at Gotham Cemetery.

Catwoman nudged Batman.

"Perfect night for a date, don't you think?" Catwoman said. "Two masked vigilantes on the prowl, beneath a full moon, with homicidal villains lurking in the shadows . . ."

Batman pulled an earpiece from his Utility Belt. "Contact me using this."

Catwoman put the earpiece in. "Yes, sir," she said with a sarcastic salute. "Any other orders, Captain Batman?"

"Just one," Batman said. He looked right at her. "Stay safe."

Catwoman's eyes went wide. "I didn't know you cared," she said quietly.

Without another word, Catwoman headed into the graveyard. Batman watched her go. After a moment, he joined her in the shadows.

CHAPTER 4

GOTHAM CEMETERY

Sticking to the shadows, Catwoman led Batman through Gotham Cemetery. It was an eerie, old place. Many of the structures and graves were badly deteriorated. Some gravestones were no longer legible.

Batman kept his eyes open for clues while Catwoman checked her handheld device. Suddenly she stopped. "That's odd," she said. "The signal indicates he's right below us."

"A tracking device?" Batman asked, already knowing the answer.

Catwoman frowned. "Yes," she said. "But it seems to have stopped working."

Batman pointed at the archway above the mausoleum. Catwoman narrowed her eyes. There was a black skull engraved in the marble.

Catwoman smiled. "Who says bats are blind?" she joked. "I'll bet that Black Mask is beneath this mausoleum."

They approached the heavy stone doors. Batman gestured with his hand. "Ladies first," he said with a half-bow.

Catwoman flashed a smile. As quick as a shot, she kicked open the doors. *CRRRRRRRREAK!* Moonlight spilled inside the marble building, illuminating the dust that fell from above. They watched it settle on the shoulders of two figures in the center of the room.

Both of the men were wearing masks with strange lenses in the eyepieces. "Just two of them?" Catwoman said in a pouty voice. "I'll take the one on the left." She charged inside the building.

"Wait!" Batman said. But she didn't listen. He had no choice but to follow her.

CLANK! The doors closed behind them. The room was plunged into complete darkness. "Oops," Catwoman said.

"Two more behind us," Batman told her.

"And I bet those lenses in their masks are for night vision," Catwoman added.

CLICK-CLICK! Batman and Catwoman simultaneously activated their night-vision lenses. Batman looked up just in time to dive away from a huge marble pillar falling straight toward him. **KRRRUNCH!**

The pillar smashed into the marble floor and shattered. Batman saw the biggest False Facer charge at him. As the thug wrapped his thick arms around Batman, he saw the crook was wearing a bull mask — and he was incredibly strong.

The thug lifted Batman onto his shoulder and slammed him into the wall. *THUD!* Batman tensed his back muscles to absorb the blow, then brought his head down onto the thug's mask. **CRUNCH!** As it broke in half, the man released his iron grip and fell to the floor in a heap.

Immediately, a second False Facer with a monkey-faced mask leaped through the air. He kicked Batman in the chest. *THA-WHUMP!* A flurry of punches followed, most of them glancing off Batman's arms and shoulders.

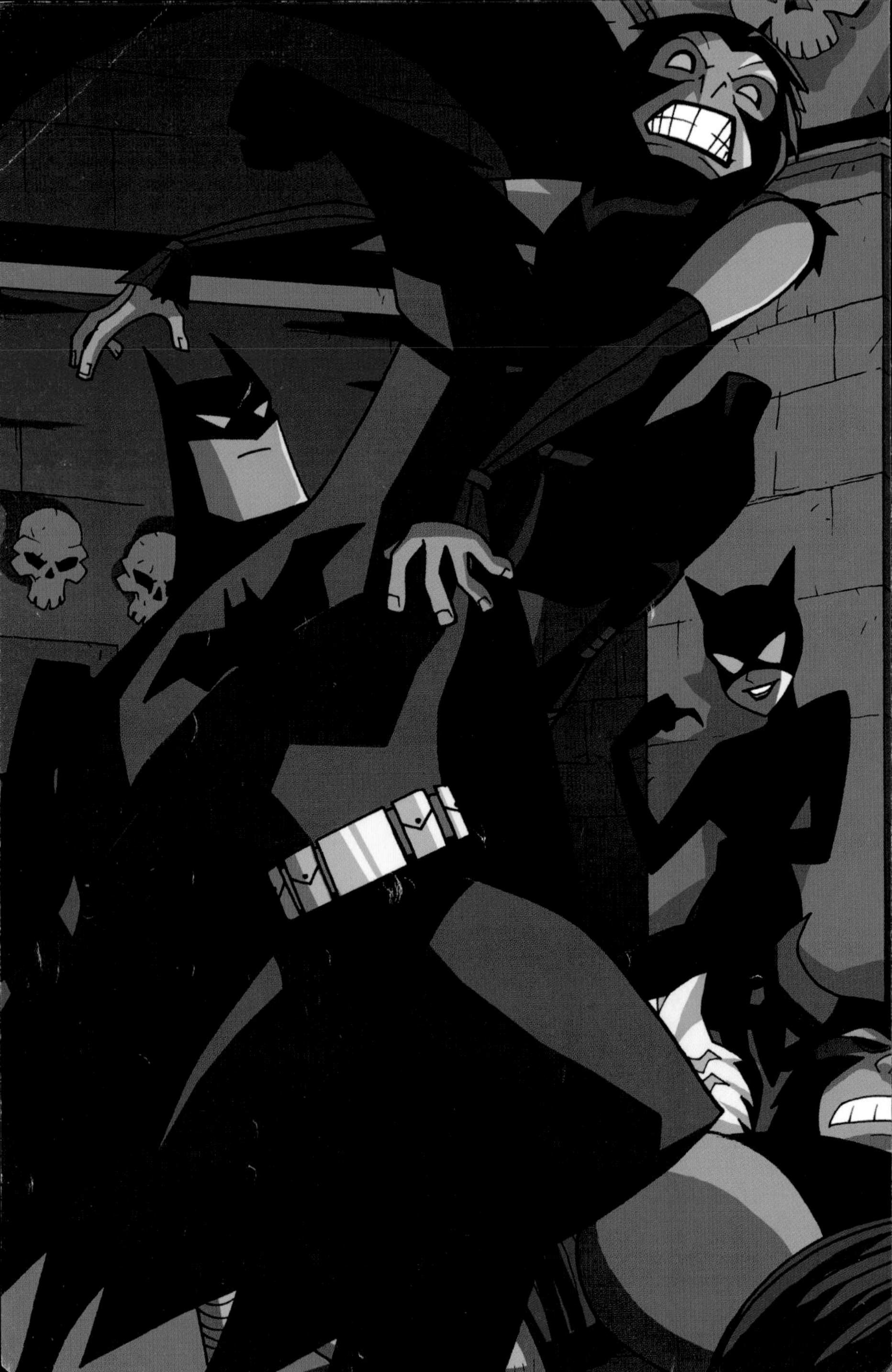

The hero sidestepped to put the crook's back to the wall. Sensing he was being cornered, the thug tossed a lunging kick at Batman to back him off. The Dark Knight deflected the blow with his wrist, knocking the agile thug off balance. **WHAM!** Batman's uppercut sent the False Facer crashing into the wall. His mask fell to the ground as the thug slumped down hard.

Batman spun around, prepared to help Catwoman fight the remaining False Facers. However, he found her leaning casually against a pillar.

"What took you so long?" she asked. The two other thugs were near her feet and tied up with thin black rope.

"Nicely done," Batman said. "But next time, try to be a little more cautious."

Catwoman put her hands on her hips and frowned. It reminded Batman of Selina's posture when he left her back at the ball. "Fine," she said. "Then you lead."

Batman glanced around the chamber. There didn't seem to be any doors, aside from the front entry. He approached the rear wall and ran his hands along it. "A dead end?" he muttered to himself.

Catwoman snickered. "Interesting choice of words." Casually, she walked over to the wall and yanked on a skeletal mask above Batman's head. **CLICK!** It swung to the left.

RUMBLE! Batman leaped back as the stone wall parted. Inside was a dank, musty hallway leading down into the darkness.

Batman glanced at Catwoman in disbelief. "How did you —?"

"There's heat coming up from beneath that wall," she said. "Don't your goggles have infrared vision?"

Batman grinned. "You want to take the lead back?"

Catwoman walked toward the hidden passageway and playfully pushed the Dark Knight toward the secret entrance. "I think I made my point," she said.

Batman crossed his arms. "You wish."

Catwoman chuckled as she followed Batman down the stairs.

They descended what seemed like countless steps until they reached a long, dark tunnel at the bottom. They saw a small source of light at the end of the tunnel, which opened into what looked like a very large room made of stone.

"That, my friend, is a bottleneck," Catwoman said.

"Agreed," Batman said. "I'll go first."

"What if it's a trap?" Catwoman asked.

Batman smiled. "It probably is. And you're going to be the ace up my sleeve." He pointed upward. There was a gap in the stone between the wall and the ceiling.

"So, you trust me?" Catwoman asked.

"I trust your *instincts*," Batman said. And with that, he entered the dark corridor and headed toward the light at the end of the tunnel while Catwoman scurried up onto the ledge and into the darkness.

* * *

After a few minutes of walking, Batman emerged into a giant arena-like chamber.

Several flaming torches illuminated the entire scene. Stone seats were carved into the stone along the side walls. They all surrounded a throne-like chair at the front and center of the seats. It reminded Batman of a small stadium. *Or a gladiator pit,* he thought grimly.

Batman looked around the room. There weren't any exits or doors. "I think I've hit a dead end," he said to Catwoman through his earpiece. "Any luck on your end?"

"No sign of the donation money yet," Catwoman said.

"What about Gordon?" Batman asked.

"Nope," Catwoman said. "But I wasn't really looking for him."

Suddenly, a loud **CLANK!** came from behind Batman.

A cast-iron gate now blocked the entrance. Batman's eyes scanned the arena. "Catwoman, I'm going to need some backup," he whispered. He looked up at the gap above the gate, hoping to see Selina waiting in the shadows. But all he saw was darkness.

"Catwoman?" Batman repeated. He waited for a response.

HAHAHAHA! A laugh echoed through the chamber. Batman turned to see Black Mask emerge from behind the central throne.

The villain threw his hands up in the air. "Welcome, Batman!" he yelled, his voice reverberating. "We're glad you could join our little party."

One by one, masked faces emerged from behind the seats in the arena.

In a matter of moments, all the seats were filled with False Facers, all their eyes fixed on Batman.

"Kind of overkill, don't you think?" Batman said, gesturing at the many masked thugs.

Black Mask shrugged. "I'm not taking any chances with you."

"Where's Gordon?" Batman growled.

Black Mask leaned to his side. Casually, he pointed his finger toward the ceiling. **KLANK·A·KLANK!** Slowly, rung-by-rung, a chain holding a human-sized birdcage descended from a hole in the ceiling. It stopped about twenty feet above the floor. Inside sat Police Commissioner Gordon. He looked miserable.

Batman tensed. "I take it you've been expecting me," he said to Black Mask.

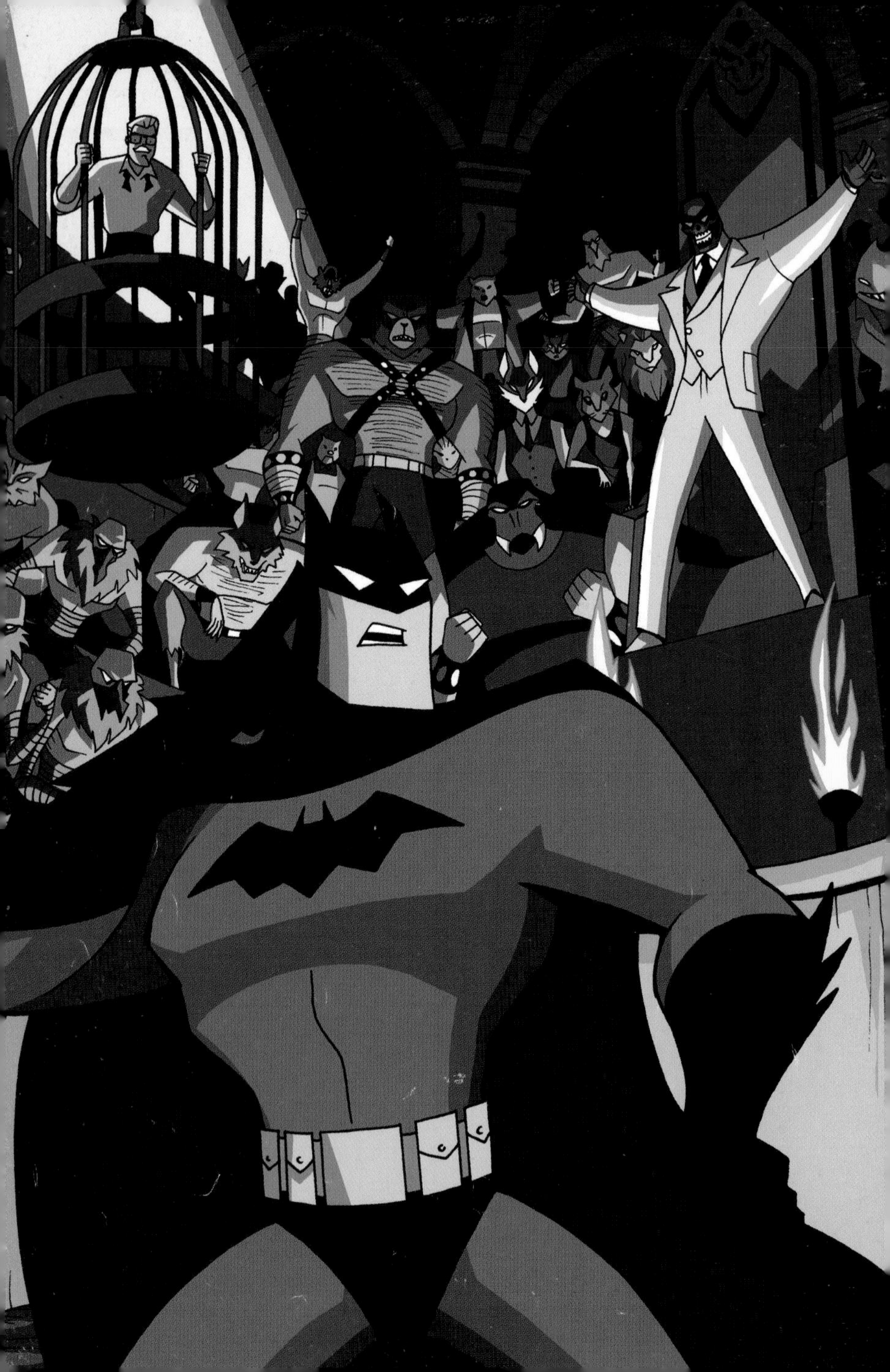

Black Mask approached the edge of the pit. "I didn't exactly conceal my tracks," he said with a grin. "But I admit, you found me faster than I expected. Thankfully, most of my men were already here."

Batman glanced around the arena, finding cold gazes staring back at him from behind beastly masks. "Now would be a good time to drop in, Catwoman," he whispered. But still, he got no response.

"I'd like to thank you for making my job so easy," Black Mask continued. "With Two-Face and the Penguin gone, I have no criminal competition left. With Gordon in my grasp, the police are helpless, and my False Facers outnumber them five to one. And now —"

"I'm your only obstacle to criminal supremacy," Batman interrupted.

"Exactly," the villain said. He held his palm out toward Batman. "However, I am willing to offer you a deal."

"And that would be?" Batman asked.

The villain's lips curled into a chilling grin. It seemed as if the mask itself was smiling. "Just take off your mask," he said. "And I'll let you live."

Batman knew that wasn't an option. It would put all his friends in harm's way, as well as jeopardize his ability to protect Gotham. "Not going to happen," he said.

Black Mask frowned. "But why?" he asked. "Granted, your career as a masked vigilante would be over, and you'd probably end up in jail . . . but you'd still be alive." He ran a finger along his neck in a cutting motion. "Isn't that better than the alternative?"

Batman said nothing. *POP! POP! POP!*
Instead, he cracked his knuckles.

Black Mask crossed his arms. "Fine,"
he said. "I'll just unmask you when you're
dead."

Black Mask snapped his fingers. *CLICK!*
Two False Facers leaped into the pit. "Let
the Black Masquerade begin!" he cried.

The crowd of thugs cheered wildly.

CHAPTER 5

THE BLACK MASQUERADE

Two False Facers stalked toward the Dark Knight. Batman saw that the first thug was wearing a bear mask, and he was big. As he lumbered forth, Batman noted his feet landed heavily on the stone floor.

The second thug wore a snake-like mask. He stood behind and to the side of the bear thug, and held a club in his right hand. His posture was low and tense, as if preparing for the perfect opportunity to strike.

The big thug charged at Batman with his hands open. *He wants to grab me so his little pal can finish me,* Batman realized.

The Dark Knight rolled underneath
the bear man's legs. The thug stumbled
forward in an attempt to grab Batman and
almost fell on his face.

Before the smaller thug could react,
Batman jumped toward him with his knee
extended. *KA·THUMP!* His knee hit the thug
in the chest, knocking him to the stone
floor. His club skittered away, out of reach.

Batman knew what would come next.
WOOSH! He ducked, narrowly avoiding
the bigger man's attempt to grab him from
behind. Staying low, Batman swept the
man's feet with a kick. The villain hit the
ground with a *THUD!*

At that moment, the snake thug leaped
onto Batman's back and wrapped his arms
around Batman's face. "I've got him!" he
hissed. "Quick, put his lights out!"

Batman could have easily thrown the crook over his shoulders. Instead, he pretended to struggle — until he saw the bigger thug wind up for a powerful punch.

Batman shrugged and ducked at the same time. The bear thug's fist smashed into the smaller one's mask. **CRUNCH!** The mask split in half, and the snake thug was down for the count.

Batman leaped onto the bigger thug's back. He wrapped his elbow under the man's chin and wound his legs around his waist. Then he squeezed with all his might.

The False Facer grabbed at Batman's cape, trying to pull the hero off his back. But it was no use. In moments, his limbs went limp and he fell to the floor, asleep.

BOOOOOOOOOOOOOOO! A chorus of jeers rang out. **BOOOOOOOOOO!**

AROOOOOOOOOOO! Suddenly, one thug let out a dramatic howl that silenced the rest. He wore a mask that resembled a snarling wolf. As he stood, the False Facers near him slowly backed away.

Then the man leaped into the arena from the fourth row. *THUMP!* He landed on all fours right in front of Black Mask's throne. He lowered his head in the throne's direction, as if silently asking to take on the Dark Knight.

Black Mask seemed pleased. "I like your initiative, Wolf," he said. "You have my permission."

Wolf didn't hesitate. He dashed toward Batman, covering the distance between them in a matter of seconds. *WHAM!* A strong arm smashed into Batman's head, knocking him to the side.

Just as Batman regained his balance, Wolf knocked him onto his back, then pounced on his chest. He sent flurries of wild punches to Batman's body and head.

Batman was able to block most of the blows, but more and more were getting through. He tried to wiggle free, but Wolf had his full weight on Batman's chest. The thug threw punch after punch after punch.

Batman felt a stinging sensation in the back of his neck. *I never should've trusted Selina,* he thought.

Suddenly, a loud snapping sound echoed through the chamber. **KA·RACK!** A black rope wrapped around Wolf's throat. He brought his hands to his neck, trying to pull it free. But it was far too tight. The man was pulled back, taking pressure off Batman's chest.

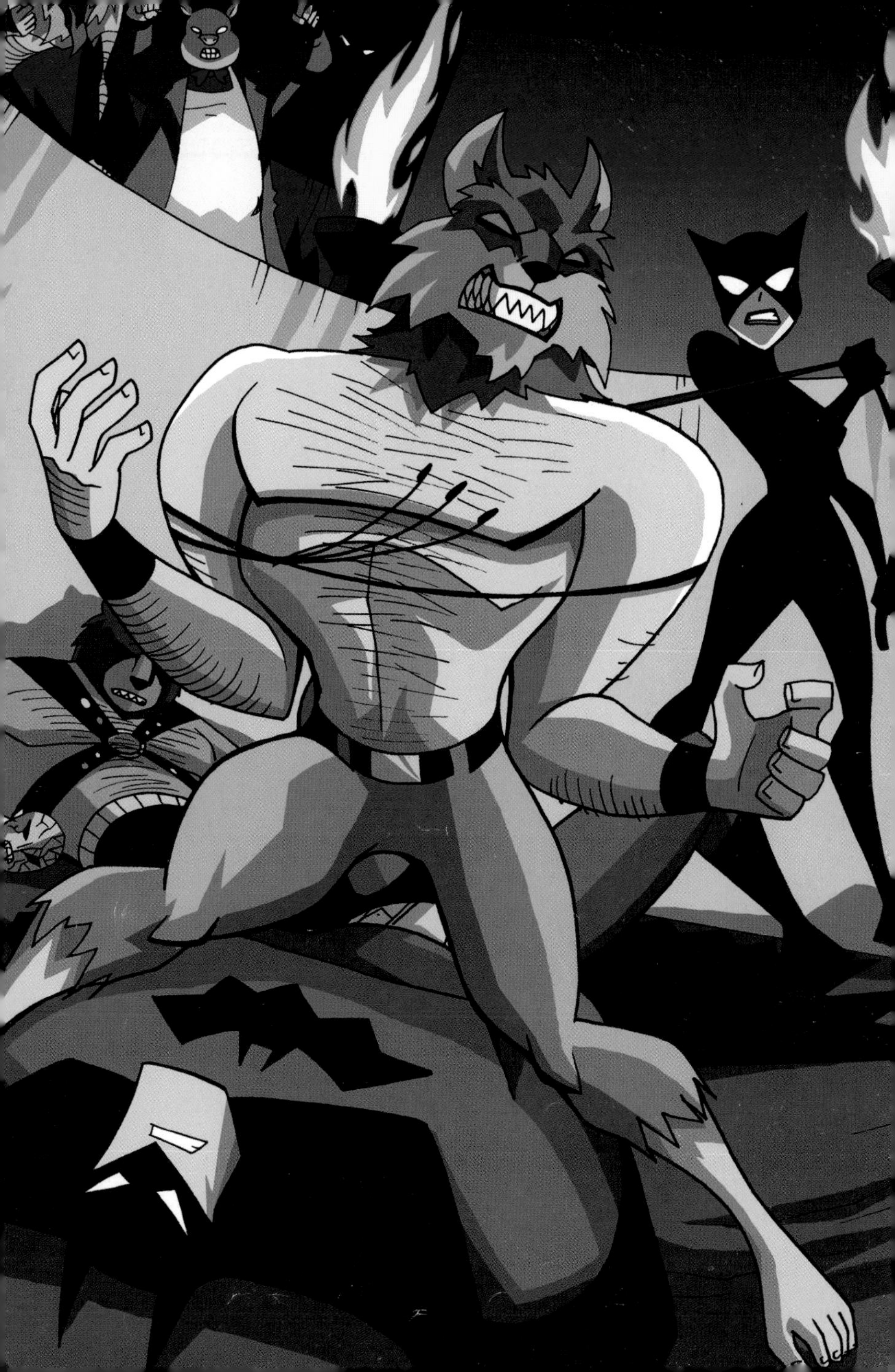

Batman slid his legs free. **THUMP!** He kicked Wolf onto his back.

Batman sprang to his feet to see Catwoman tying the wolf thug's wrists together with a zip-tie. Batman glanced at her, uncertain what to say.

Catwoman tilted her head. "Cat got your tongue?"

Batman grinned. "Thanks, Catwoman."

"Don't thank me yet," she said, recoiling her whip. "I think we're just getting started."

Black Mask laughed. "How cute," he said. "Two masked vigilantes teaming up. Who wants to finish them off?"

Several angry voices pleaded Black Mask for the opportunity to fight. "Let me at him!" came a voice from a lion mask.

"Let us tear him apart!" cried a man wearing a vulture mask. Batman saw four other thugs wearing identical masks sitting next to him. They nodded in unison.

"No!" bellowed a portly thug. Batman saw he was wearing what looked like a walrus mask. "He's mine!"

The walrus thug approached the ledge of the pit. He tried to swing his leg over and jump down, but it got caught on the edge. He tumbled over the side. **THUMP!** He landed face first on the stone floor.

The False Facers snickered. Black Mask, however, did not look pleased. "Help him!" he yelled at the five vultures.

As one, the vultures swooped into the pit and surrounded the walrus. They helped him climb to his feet. Then, together, they attacked Batman and Catwoman.

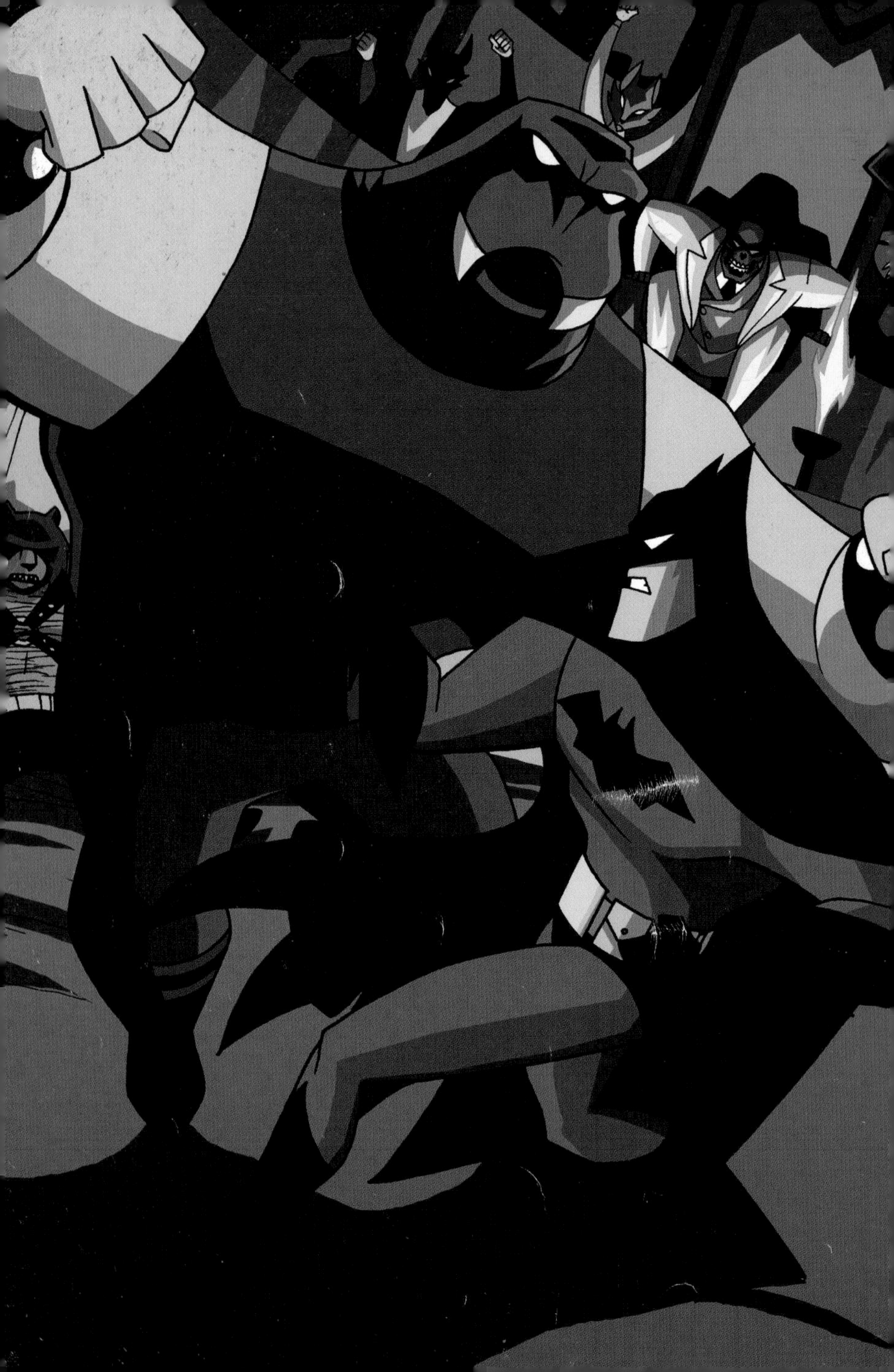

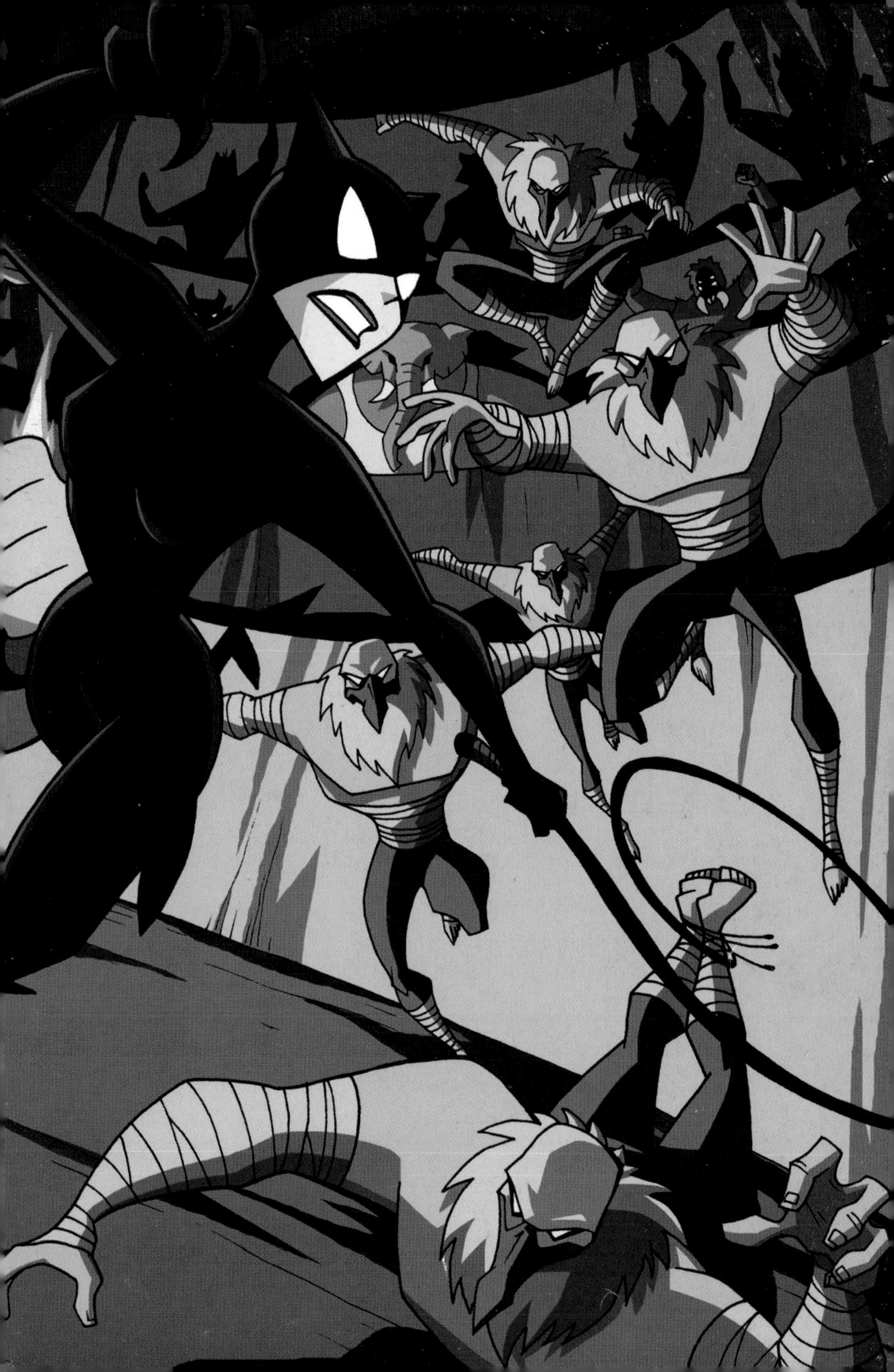

Catwoman swung her whip at one of the vultures. **CRACK!** It latched onto his leg, tripping him to the ground. The second vulture jumped on the whip with both his feet, trapping it against the floor, while the tripped vulture freed his leg from the whip.

Another vulture's bony fist sailed toward her face. **WOOSH!** She deftly wrapped her whip around the attacker's arm and pulled him to the floor. Immediately, two pairs of hands grabbed her and tackled her.

Batman managed to throw one of them off Catwoman before the walrus ploughed into his shoulder. **WHAM!** The large man fell on Batman's legs, pinning him to the ground. A vulture climbed up the walrus's back and peered into Batman's face. He brought his fist back for a punch, but Batman was faster.

THUNK! Batman bashed the thug over his head with his grapnel gun, then fired it toward the ceiling. *KLANK!* It attached itself to Gordon's cage. Batman was pulled up and away from the two thugs.

On the ascent, Batman released the rope. He went soaring through the air toward Catwoman and the two remaining vultures who were pummeling her. *WHAM! SMACK!* His feet connected with the vultures' backs, crumpling them against the arena's wall.

Batman helped Catwoman to her feet. She used the momentum to spring forward with a jumping kick at the charging walrus. The big thug blocked the kick with his huge arm, tossing her aside.

Batman wrapped his legs around the walrus's thigh in an attempt to trip him.

Instead, the thug just lowered his knee onto Batman's chest and held him there.

"Urk!" Batman grunted.

Catwoman leaped on the big thug's back and wrapped her whip around his neck. But the thug just threw her aside like a ragdoll. She flipped, then landed gracefully on her feet with a big smile on her face.

"What are you grinning about, lady?!" the walrus asked.

BEEP! BEEP! His eyes went to the side as he heard a noise behind his ear. Catwoman winked at Batman.

"I attached a remote explosive to your back," Catwoman told the walrus.

Then Catwoman produced a remote control from her belt. "It was nice knowing you," she said, flipping a switch. **CLICK!**

The man's eyes went wide with fear. He stood and flailed wildly in an attempt to reach his muscular arms to his back.

The Dark Knight sprang to his feet with an uppercut. **WHACK!** The walrus was no doubt down for the count.

Catwoman and Batman stood shoulder to shoulder in front of Black Mask's throne. Batman noticed that the remaining False Facers were fidgeting nervously in their seats. *Most of them are the Penguin's and Harvey's former thugs,* Batman realized.

"I'll tell you what, False Facers!" Batman said, his voice booming. "I won't throw you all in jail after I arrest your boss — if you remove your masks and leave. *Now.*"

A moment passed as the False Facers looked back and forth at each other uncertainly.

But sure enough, Batman was right —
the first to run was a False Facer with a rat-
like mask. He tossed his mask to the ground
and ran toward the far wall.

"Get back here!" Black Mask screamed.

With all his weight, the fleeing thug
pulled on an unlit torch. *CREEEEEEEAK!*
The iron gate was raised. The thug ran
through without a single glance back.

Then the other False Facers threw off
their masks and followed suit.

WHAM! Black Mask slammed his fists
on the arms of his throne. The veins in his
neck bulged out. Batman could practically
hear his teeth grinding.

"*RRROOOOAR!*" Black Mask growled.
He leaped over the edge of the pit and
charged toward the Dark Knight.

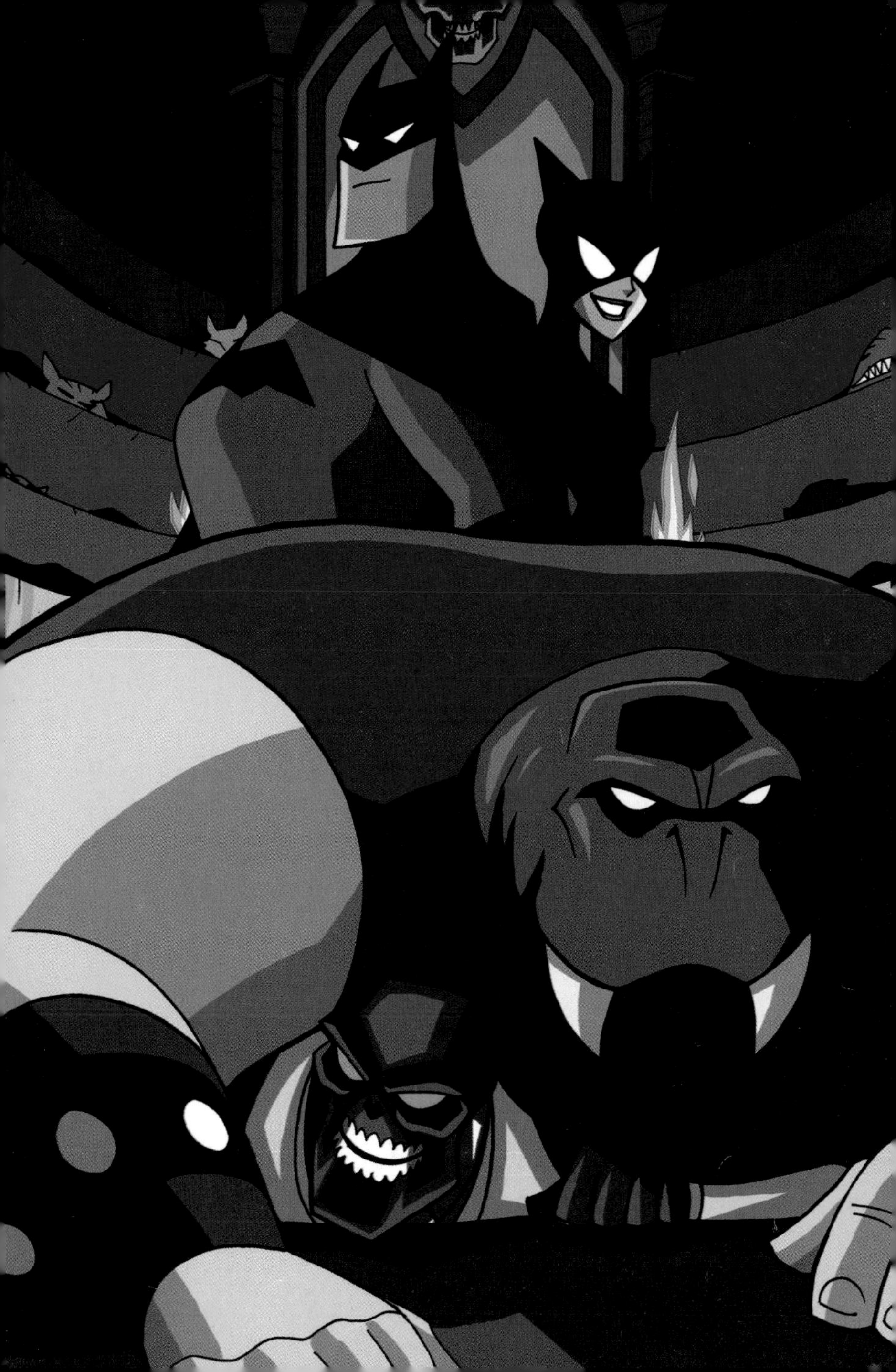

FWUMP! Both Catwoman and Batman leapt back as the walrus landed on top of Black Mask. The two fell to the ground with a sickening **THUD!**

Batman watched in shock as the walrus slowly stood. Black Mask lay on his stomach, breathing but not moving.

The walrus thug dropped his mask to the ground. "Do I get the same deal as the others?" he asked.

Batman grinned. "That depends on how fast you run," he said.

Catwoman laughed as the muscle-bound man sprinted away. Batman wrapped Black Mask's arms behind his back and secured them with a zip-tie. He checked the villain's pulse. It was slow, but steady.

"Batman!" Gordon's voiced called out from above. "The donation funds are in the compartment above me!"

Batman looked up to see Gordon had wiggled free of his bonds. "Thanks, Jim," he said. "We'll have you down shortly."

Batman glanced at Catwoman. "Would you mind bringing the donation funds back to Wayne Manor for me?"

Catwoman's eyes went wide. "You . . . trust me to do that?"

Batman nodded — and covertly produced a tracking device from his belt.

Catwoman looked upward and cracked her whip toward the cage above. **SLAP!** It attached to the cage's chain. She began to scurry upward when Batman touched her shoulder. "And thanks," he said.

Catwoman smiled from ear to ear. She scurried up the whip toward the cage. Hanging upside down from her whip, she picked the lock to Gordon's cage. Then she continued up the chain and into the hole in the ceiling, leaving her whip behind for Gordon to climb down.

Black Mask groaned. Batman watched as the villain rolled onto his side. Gone was the criminal's confidence, intensity, and rage. He looked frightened. Even his stone mask couldn't hide it.

"I'll offer you the same deal you offered me," Batman said. "Take off your mask, and I'll ask the judge to go easy on you."

Black Mask tilted his head. The ebony stone of his mask glimmered in the torchlight. "What mask?"

He's made his choice, Batman thought.

Batman nodded at Gordon. The commissioner escorted Black Mask back toward the surface.

* * *

Battered and bruised, Batman emerged from the catacombs. He wanted nothing more than to go home and rest, but he had one last thing to do.

Catwoman had come through this time. Batman had even seen Selina's personality show through her Catwoman alter ego this evening. But he'd been sure he'd gotten through to her before, only to see her return to her criminal ways. He wanted to trust her to return the money to Wayne Manor, but there was just too much at stake.

Batman reached into his Utility Belt.

Batman produced a handheld computer and activated it. **CLICK!**

A tracking beacon appeared — far from Wayne Manor.

Batman frowned.

WOOSH! He shot his grapnel gun at a nearby roof, then sailed upward to it.

Batman continued to leap from rooftop to rooftop, chasing after Catwoman from above, growing more angry and disappointed with each shot.

Then the tracking beacon stopped moving.

Batman glanced over the edge of the roof he was currently on. Down below, he saw Catwoman setting the donation box on the steps of the Gotham City Orphanage.

Then Catwoman stood up, pressed the doorbell, and scurried into a nearby alley.

Batman smiled. "Thanks, Catwoman," he said, hoping she'd kept her earpiece in.

After a moment, Selina's voice said, "Until next time, Batman."

THE BLACK MASK

REAL NAME:
Roman Sionis

OCCUPATION:
Crimelord

BASE:
Gotham City

HEIGHT:
6 feet, 1 inch

WEIGHT:
195 pounds

EYES:
Red

HAIR:
None

Despite growing up as a son of a wealthy family, Roman Sionis had a difficult childhood. He was dropped on his head at birth, mostly ignored by his parents, and bitten by a rabid raccoon. One day, eager to escape his miserable life, Roman donned a mask made of stone and recruited Gotham's criminals into his gang, the False Face Society. From that day foward, he became known as the Black Mask — one of the most feared and

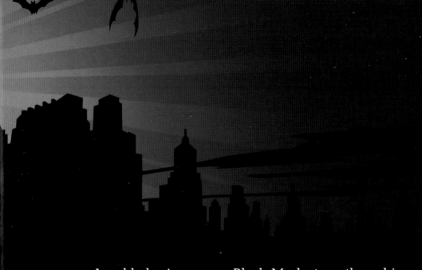

- An able businessman, Black Mask strengthens his grip over Gotham with ill-gotten corporate gains from the Janus Corporation.

- Black Mask once evaded capture at the hands of the Dark Knight by escaping through the false bottom of a coffin.

- Black Masks runs his False Face Society from the underground crypts in Gotham City.

- Roman Sionis fashioned his black mask out of ebony stone from the pieces of a broken casket. Then he abandoned his former identity and wholly embraced his Black Mask persona.

BIOGRAPHIES

SEAN TULIEN is a children's book editor living and working in Minnesota. In his spare time, he likes to spend time with his lovely fiancée, read, eat sushi, exercise outdoors, listen to loud music, play with animals, and write books like this one.

LUCIANO VECCHIO was born in 1982 and currently lives in Buenos Aires, Argentina. With experience in illustration, animation, and comics, his works have been published in the US, Spain, UK, France, and Argentina. His credits include *Ben 10* (DC Comics), *Cruel Thing* (Norma), *Unseen Tribe* (Zuda Comics), and *Sentinels* (Drumfish Productions).

GLOSSARY

catacombs (KAT-uh-kohmz)—an underground cemetery consisting of many tunnels and rooms

charisma (kuh-RIZ-muh)—powerful personal appeal

cryptic (KRIP-tik)—mysterious or puzzling

egotistical (ee-guh-TISS-ti-kuhl)—obsessed with oneself

elude (i-LUDE)—to escape or get away from someone

henchmen (HENCH-muhn)—thugs or criminals who are obedient to, or take orders from, a leader

masquerade (mass-kuh-RADE)—to pretend to be something you are not, or a party at which all the people dress up and wear masks

mausoleum (maw-zuh-LEE-uhm)—a large building that houses a tomb or tombs

silhouette (sil-oo-ET)—a dark outline seen against a light background

sinister (SIN-uh-stur)—seeming evil and threatening

testimony (TESS-tuh-moh-nee)—a statement given by a witness who is under oath in a court of law

vigilante (vij-uh-LAN-tee)—any person who takes the law into their own hands

DISCUSSION QUESTIONS

1. Catwoman and Batman team up to take down the Black Mask. Which hero played a bigger role in defeating the super-villain? Discuss your answers.

2. Why do you think Black Mask's men abandoned him? Explain your answer using specific examples from the text.

3. This book has ten illustrations. Which one is your favorite? Why?

WRITING PROMPTS

1. Black Mask's men betrayed him. Have you ever felt betrayed by someone? Have you ever let someone else down? Write about your experience.

2. Do you think Batman could've beaten Black Mask without Catwoman's help? Why or why not? Use examples from the text to support your answer.

3. Create your own False Facer! What kind of mask do they wear? What are their strengths and weaknesses? Write a few paragraphs about your villain, then draw a picture of him or her.

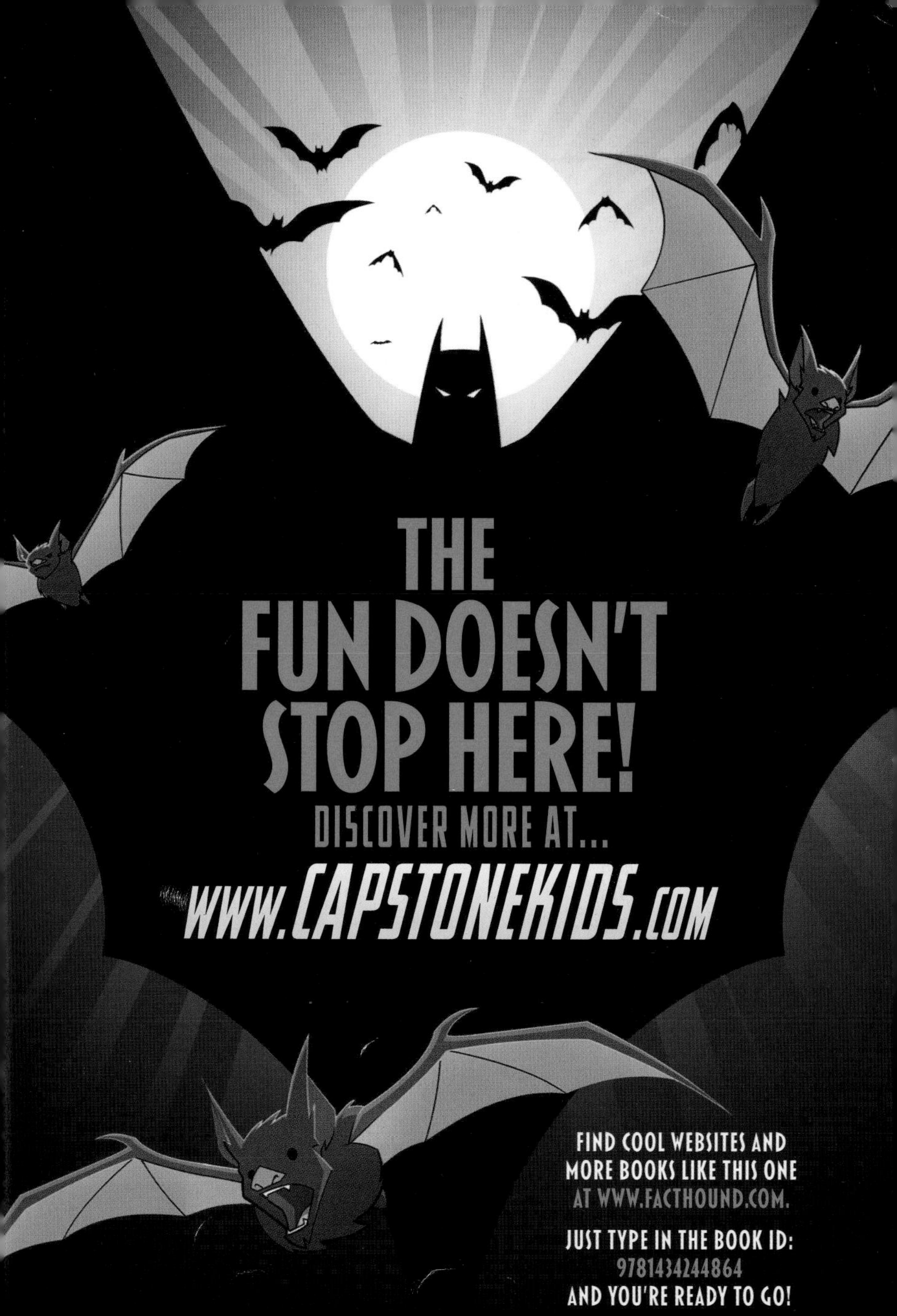
THE
FUN DOESN'T
STOP HERE!
DISCOVER MORE AT...
WWW.CAPSTONEKIDS.COM
FIND COOL WEBSITES AND
MORE BOOKS LIKE THIS ONE
AT WWW.FACTHOUND.COM.
JUST TYPE IN THE BOOK ID:
9781434244864
AND YOU'RE READY TO GO!

LOOK FOR MORE

THE DARK KNIGHT™

SUPER DC HEROES
THE DARK KNIGHT
DANGER ON DECK
SONNEBORN · VECCHIO

SUPER DC HEROES
THE DARK KNIGHT
BATMAN UNDERCOVER
WEISSBURG · LEVINS

SUPER DC HEROES
THE DARK KNIGHT
THE PENGUIN'S CRIME WAVE
SUTTON · VECCHIO

SUPER DC HEROES
THE DARK KNIGHT
THE BLACK MASQUERADE
TULIEN · VECCHIO

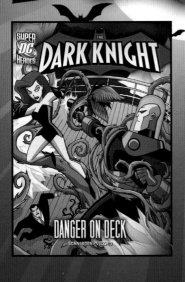